The Great Leaf Blast-Off

BY JOHN HIMMELMAN

Silver Press

For Joanie, one of the all time greatest
sister-in-laws!

—J.H.

Library of Congress Cataloging-in-Publication Data

Himmelman, John.
 The great leaf blast-off! / story and pictures by John Himmelman.
 p. cm.—(The Fix-it family)
 Summary: Relates the amusing adventures of a family of inventors.
 [1. Inventors—Fiction. 2. Family life—Fiction. 3. Moles
 (Animals)—Fiction.] I. Title. II. Series: Himmelman, John,
 Fix-it family.
PZ7.H5686Gr 1990
[E]—dc20   90-8122
ISBN 0-671-69634-3 (lib. bdg.)   CIP
ISBN 0-671-69638-6 (pbk.)   AC

Produced by Small Packages, Inc.
Published by Silver Press, a division of
Silver Burdett Press, Inc.
Simon & Schuster, Inc.,
Prentice Hall Bldg., Englewood Cliffs, NJ 07632.
Printed in the United States of America.
10 9 8 7 6 5 4 3 2 1

The Fix-it Family

Orville and Willa Wright

own a fix-it shop.

If something is broken,

they will repair it.

They can fix anything!

They are also inventors.

And their children—

Alexander, Graham, and Belle—

like inventing things, too.

CHAPTER ONE
Rake, Rake, Rake

It was a cool autumn morning.

Alexander and Graham

wanted to fly their new kites.

"Let's take them to the meadow,"

said Alexander.

They ran to the door.

"Where are you going?" asked Willa.

"To the meadow," they said.

"Did you forget what day it is today?"
she said.

"Kite flying day?" asked Graham.

"Nice try," said Willa.

"Today is Saturday.

You promised to rake the leaves."

"But that will take all day!"

said the boys.

"Not if you get started right away,"

said Willa.

Alexander and Graham went to the yard.

They started raking the leaves.

"Rake, rake, rake," said Alexander.

"Yuck, yuck, yuck," said Graham.

"There has to be a faster way."

"Yes," said Alexander.

"I am going to invent one."

"Me, too," said Graham.

Alexander had a great idea.

He borrowed his mother's hair dryer.

Graham had a great idea, too.

He borrowed the vacuum cleaner

from the fix-it shop.

They both worked on their inventions.

When they were finished,

they met in the yard.

"What is that thing?" asked Graham.

"It is my super leaf blower,"

said Alexander.

"Well mine is a super SUPER leaf eater,"

said Graham.

Alexander turned on his leaf blower.

It pushed away a few leaves.

"It is just warming up,"

said Alexander.

He turned a knob on the machine.

Now the air came out too fast.

The blower went out of control.

It started blowing the leaves

off the trees!

"Help! I can't stop this thing!"

shouted Alexander.

Graham turned off the blower.

"Do not worry," he told his brother.

"*My* machine will clean up this mess.

I am a true genius."

He turned on his leaf eater.

It ate up the leaves.

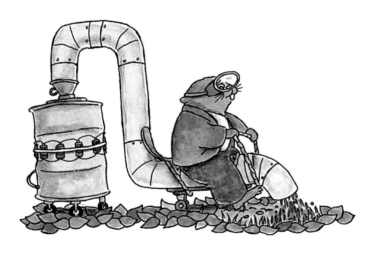

It ate up the grass.

11

It ate up the dirt.

"Turn it off

before it eats up the world!"

shouted Alexander.

They looked at the yard.

It was a mess.

"Now what?" asked Graham.

"Rake, rake, rake," said Alexander.

"Rake, rake, rake," said Graham.

CHAPTER TWO
Belle the Space Girl

Belle was bored.

Her mother was in the shower.

Her father was in the fix-it shop.

Her brothers were raking the yard.

Belle took out her favorite book.

It was all about outer space.

"I wish I had a spaceship,"

she said.

Belle looked in the garage.

There was no spaceship.

She sat on her tricycle.

"This will be my spaceship," she said.

"I will be Belle the space girl."

But her tricycle didn't look

like a spaceship.

It needed spaceship parts.

Belle left the garage

and began her search.

Willa was done with her shower.

She dried herself off.

She put on her robe.

Then she reached for the hair dryer.

It was gone!

Willa looked upstairs and downstairs.

It was nowhere in sight.

"I guess this family

needs a new hair dryer,"

she said.

"It might be fun to make one."

She got right to work.

Soon she had built a new hair dryer!

"It is a little big," she said.

"But it should do the job."

Willa brought it to the bathroom.

She looked in the mirror.

"What a mess I am!" she said.

She took another shower

and dried herself off, again.

She put on her robe, again.

She reached for the hair dryer, again.

It was gone, again!

"Something funny is going on here,"

she said.

Orville finished his work for the day.

"I hope the Frogleys

like this new fly catcher I made,"

he said.

"I can't wait to show it to them."

Orville put away all his tools.

But the floor was still a mess.

He went to get his shop vacuum.

It wasn't there!

"I must have lent it to the neighbors,"

he thought.

"No problem. I will just invent

something else to clean the floor."

He got all his tools back out.

Then he collected bits and pieces

of this and that for the invention.

Soon it was finished.

"And now for the test," he said.

"But first I have to

put my tools away."

When he was done,

he was ready to vacuum the floor.

He looked for his invention.

It was not in the shop!

"This time, I am sure

I didn't lend it to the neighbors,"

he said.

CHAPTER THREE
Blast Off!

"Can you fly a kite in the dark?"
asked Graham.

"Why?" asked Alexander.

"Because it will be dark
before we finish raking these leaves,"
said Graham.

Half of the day was over.

Half of the leaves

were still on the ground.

The boys raked faster.

Then Graham stopped.

He heard a strange noise.

CLACKITTY, CLACK, CLACK.

It came from the garage.

"What was that?" asked Graham.

The boys ran over to the garage.

"LOOK OUT!" shouted Alexander.

A strange machine raced past them.

Belle was sitting on top of it.

"BLAST OFF!" she shouted.

She pedaled her spaceship
into the yard.
It had her father's invention
on the front.
And it had her mother's invention
on the back.

She headed toward a pile of leaves.

"Hey, watch out!" shouted Graham.

"Silly earth people," said Belle.

The leaves flew straight up in the air.

"Pretty stars!" she said.

"Make more stars! Make more stars!"

shouted the boys.

Belle pedaled her spaceship

back and forth across the yard.

Soon every leaf was gone.

"No more stars," she said sadly.

"NO MORE LEAVES!"

cheered Alexander and Graham.

"Welcome back to earth, Belle."

"I am not Belle," she said.

"I am a space girl."

Willa and Orville came to the door.

"So that is what happened
to my hair dryers," said Willa.

"And my vacuums," said Orville.

"The yard is clean.

Can we play now?" asked Graham.

"After you put away what you borrowed,"

said Orville.

Alexander took apart his invention
and put back the hair dryer.

Graham took apart *his* invention
and put back the shop vacuum.

They picked up their kites

and started to run to the meadow.

Then they stopped.

They ran back to the house.

"Come on, Belle," said Alexander.

"It will be good to have a space girl

help us fly our kites."

Belle smiled.

They all hurried to the meadow.

"I wonder what they did
with all the leaves," said Willa.
"I am sure they found
a good place for them,"
said Orville.

The End